You & Your Dad

by Lou Alpert

 Whispering Coyote Press   Dallas

Published by Whispering Coyote Press
300 Crescent Court, Suite 860, Dallas, TX 75201

Book production and design by *The Kids at Our House*
10 9 8 7 6 5 4 3 2
Printed in Hong Kong

Library of Congress Cataloging-in-Publication Data

Alpert, Lou.
You & your dad / by Lou Alpert.
p.   cm.
Summary: Depicts many kinds of fathers and the activities they
share with their children.
ISBN 1-879085-36-4 (hardcover): $14.95
1. Father and child—Juvenile literature.   [1. Father and child.]
I. Title.   II. Title: You and your dad.
HQ755.85.A435   1992
306.874′2—dc20   91-44412   CIP   AC

*Love and love to
Ian and Spence*

What kind of dad spends time with you?

Where does he work? What does he do?

Does he work in an office that reaches the sky?

Does he wear overalls
or a coat and a tie?

Does he leave in a train or drive in a car?

Where does he go
when he leaves
for the day—

a hospital, store,
or a boat in a bay,

a taxi, a school,

or a city subway?

Does he drive a tractor,

talk on the phone?

At the end of the day when his work is all done,

what is it you and
your dad do for fun?

Do you like to go running or work on old cars,

or lie on the grass
and just look at the stars?

Do you listen to music
and dance down the hall,

or practice catching
and throwing a ball?

Do you go to the movies

or read a
good book,

play in the garden,

swing,

swim, or cook?

Do you play in the snow

or just take a nap,

go to the opera
or rock in his lap?

Do you work on
a tree house or
help wash the car,

travel and see things in
lands that are far?

Do you go to a ball game or

watch the TV,

Do you like to have picnics or go out to eat

at a restaurant in town or a stand on the street?

When nighttime has fallen and your day is done,

you can sit with your
daddy and share all your fun.

Wherever you go and whatever you do,
your dad is special and so are you!